Prologue

My bright green eyes shined back at me while I
brushed my long, blond hair in the mirror as I looked over
my fair and pinkish skin. My father always said I looked
like a china doll.
I laughed at the thought.
I am very thin with amazing curves with my C cup breasts.
My height is where I am short, standing about 5'1. As
perfect as this might sound I am not so perfect. I have a
secret that I can never tell; it is a blessing and a curse. As
you will find out, I am the only one in my family with
green eyes and short height. Nothing unusual there, but
when I got really mad at my brother when I was ten, I
found out how different I was truly was. I did something I
knew was not normal. I ran to my room and slammed my
door. I stood there with my eyes closed; my fists squeezed
so tight, drawing blood. I couldn't understand why I was so
mad but I couldn't calm down. Heat began flowing through
my body. It was like slowly dipping myself in hot water, it
just crawled through me. After a few seconds I opened my
eyes and I stifled a scream. I looked around as my body
shook, not sure how to take in the sight before me. My
stuffed animals, clothes, junk…everything was floating in
midair. I reached out with a shaky hand to touch it. When
my hand touched the bear I jerked back. I didn't know what
was going on or what to believe. I was hoping this was a
nightmare. I gathered my courage together. I grabbed the

stuffed bear and pulled it down. I had no idea it was me
doing this at first. I closed my eyes and relaxed, taking
deep breaths trying to calm down. A cooling sensation ran
over me and when I reopened my eyes everything that was
floating, started to sink back to the floor. I sat there
freaking out. I looked at the bear I was holding. I pushed
with everything I had...nothing happened. Nothing
happened for a long time. I had to keep that secret to
myself but it haunted me every day. I couldn't ask someone
what was wrong with me for the fear of them thinking I
was crazy. Finally, I met someone who was different like
me. I was on vacation with my family at the beach. I
walked outside with my brothers and they drifted off, busy
finding girls. When I went to the water's edge a girl walked
up beside me and smiled. I felt like I knew her, like we had
met before but I knew that was impossible. When our eyes
met I noticed she has the prettiest green eyes, like mine.
Those eyes held knowledge beyond her years.

"You shouldn't be out this late, you know."
I looked at her, confused as her voice broke through my
thoughts.
"I'm sorry I don't understand what you mean."
"I know what you are and your kind are almost extinct. If
they know there is even just one left they will hunt you to
the end of the earth."
I continued to look at her. I decided maybe I should walk
away. I looked around for my brothers and back to her.
"I'm sorry, you must have me confused with someone else"
She looked at me with concern, "You don't know, do you?"
"Know what?" I looked at her ready to sprint away if I
needed to. I was frightened and she stepped forward. Fear

ran though me and an all too familiar feeling entered my body.

"No, it's alright. Its ok, I'm not here to hurt you. I know what you're feeling it was strange the first time I felt it to, the burning feeling. It's ok though, its normal for us but you need to control it. You are more powerful that you could ever imagine." She simply smiled and walked away. After years of research and practice, I figured out she was right. I understand now and know I am different but will never be able to tell anyone for I am a hunted, endangered species.

I am a pixie

Chapter 1

"Hey, ready to go?"
I jumped not expecting Abby to come out of nowhere. She was always cute with her skinny jeans and tank top look. She always wore makeup that matches her deep blue eyes. She was very pretty. She definitely took after my dad with brown hair, blue eyes. She had an average body type. Not to heavy but not too thin either. You would never guess us to be sisters with my blond hair, green eyes, and short petite body.
"Yea, let's hit the road I suppose." I smiled at her. She had to drive me everywhere since she was the oldest girl. Oh, I have four brothers and one sister. You will learn about them down the road. "So, any boy talk going on in my little sisters head??" She raised her eyebrows at me.
"Um no, not any worth talking about I don't ever get to see any."
I made a pretend pouty face pushing out my plump pink lips.
"This year you will since mom is allowing y'all to go to a public school, which by the way, is why we moved to a new place and all. I'm not complaining actually, it will be good to get the boys away from the city and create a better name for themselves. Instead of those "trouble-making" Ryan boys'."
Let's just say my brothers are well known around this small city for causing a little bit of trouble. Nothing really bad just trespassing, practical jokes, stuff city people don't

think is appropriate. We are moving from a small city to the wide open country in Tennessee.

"We are meeting mom and the boys at the school to meet with the new school Principle. What's it called again?"

I looked at Abby and sighed, "Mountain View High"

"Oh yea, that's it." My sister is quite the forgetful one; as long as it doesn't pertain to her anyway. She is way out of school at 24. I'm just 15 going into high school. So I am freaking out a bit, never being in a real school before this one. We were always privately tutored. So smarts is not something anyone of us lack. My brothers just tend to use it differently. I on the other hand, love the attention from my daddy. So I study a lot and make sure my grades are always perfect. I was daddy's little princess, now, I don't know what I will be."

"We're here."

My sister's voice broke into my thoughts. I looked out my window; it was like a ghost town.

"Huh, I guess everyone is inside the building."

"You gettin' out?"

I looked up at Abby. I guess I was zoned out or freaking out.

"Yea, I guess I don't have a choice."

She elbowed me and grabbed my arm.

"Let's go, I can't take in your embarrassment from in the car."

We walked out of the car and "Mountain View" was plastered above my head. I sucked in a big breath and walked in while Abby held the door impatiently. The school's mascot was the wolf. I thought it fit since we were in the middle of nowhere. The building was brown and red brick with big red doors. You walk in and it was kind of welcoming. There were a few students standing in the hallway of course the second we passed all eyes were on the new people. As we walked I noticed a boy lingering near the principal's office. He looked up and gave the cutest grin and waved at me. I smiled but felt my cheeks heat up so I looked down. Abby opened the door and I gave a quick gland back and he had the cutest smirk.

"Hu hem. Not going to goggle over the first guy we see, are we?"

I looked at my sister and couldn't believe she said that. I turned red as a beet and walked straight through the door not looking back.

"Abby, I was not goggling. I didn't want to be rude and ignore him." I shot my nose in the air and huffed off. Finally, we made it to the principal's office and Abby knocked. The door opened after a brief second and I was ushered in.

"Why, you must be Macy?" I looked up at the man I assumed to be the principle and nodded. My brothers could sense I was nervous and started snickering amongst each other. Mom smacked them and dad gave me his sweet grin. Dad was tall with brown hair and blue eyes, tall with a built figure. Mom, on the other hand was thin, still tall, with blond hair and blue eyes.

"Mr. Jefferson, these are my lovely daughters Macy and Abby. Macy will be joining your school along with Tanner and Sage."

Mr. Jefferson looked over at me with awe, "Miss Macy, you have amazing green eyes."

I blushed, "Thank you sir."

6

"Anyway, you will all be taking a scoring test to give us an idea what classes you should attend."

Tanner huffed, "So basically I'll be taking classes with my little sister."

The principle looked at Tanner, "well, with your age difference you should be in a grade or two above Miss Macy."

Tanner laughed, "You said you would be giving us a test to see what classes we should be taking and if you give her the same test you give us. She will be a grade above me and Sage. She is a freaking genius."

"Speak for yourself you nimrod. I happen to be making better grades than you." Sage sneered.

"Why you little..."

"Either way, gentlemen, we won't know till the test are given but I have faith in you all, just the same."

I giggled as he gave me a little wink

"Your tests will begin shortly. Please go to your directed cubicles and when your test appears on the computer, you may begin."

I looked at the computer and breathed in and out.

Chapter 2

        "You have got to be kidding me!"
I snickered as we got our results back from the Placement
Test. Tanner was not happy. The highest score you can
make is a 600. Sage got a 482, Tanner got a 476, I got a
600.

"Well, Miss Macy, you have made a rather impressive
score. I mean no offense to you but I had to go back and
check to make sure you didn't cheat." Mr. Jefferson
chuckled,
"I told you she was freaking smart." Tanner stated.
"Well, never the less, she will still have to be put in with
her age group. Though, she will just have college level
classes rather than regular." He said looking at me. I
nodded in understanding.

"I'm so proud of you, my little princess." I looked at my
dad. He kissed me on the head. "If you all want you can go
explore the school."
"Thank goodness." Tanner was obviously ready to get out
of the office. He was never been good with authority, hints,
why we moved. We walked out of the office and we started
down the hall. I felt a presence behind me that was familiar.
I stopped and who else would it have been but the brown
head boy I was embarrassed in front of earlier.
"Look, I am really sorry about earlier. I didn't mean to
embarrass you." His blue eyes searched my face for
emotions.

Finally I smiled, "Your fine, I am a little new around here and I was trying to be polite."

"I'm Bruce" He reached out his hand.
"Macy" I reached out to shake his hand but before I could it was smacked away.
"Making a move on my sister, are ya?"
I rolled my eyes, "Bruce, it was very nice to meet you." I turned and walked away so my brothers would leave him alone. They may seem like they don't like me but the second a guy talks to me it's like they get jealous. I could hear them walking behind me as we went down the hall. It's like they were stalking me.

DING DING
          I jumped at the noise. Classes were getting let out. Students came out of their classes, filling the halls. I got looks from all directions, good one and definitely not so good. My brothers instantly lost interest in me as the girls walked by them. I started to walk forward when I almost ran into this boy, this very tall boy. His arms were defined like a body builder, but his face was so intense. He didn't look mad, just like he couldn't figure something out. He stared down at me for the longest time. He had to have been 6'3, had dark brown eyes, brown hair, and a very dark tan. There was something almost eerie about him.
"Hey...take a pic it last longer."
I turned to see the boy I was just talking to, um, Bruce. I looked back and the tall boy just smirked and walked away, never saying anything.
I turned back to Bruce, "Uh, thanks"

"Yeah, no problem, you have to kind of ignore them, they don't do to well around strangers. It's like they almost inspect, background check, the whole nine yards."
I looked back where he was standing, "Who are they."
"Eh, I am not really shore. He and his 'family' just moved in a few years ago. There is like a bunch of them. Like, the whole town picked up and moved here or something. They stay close together and no outsider has ever gotten in there group. Like I said, they don't do well with strangers."
I made a face, "Huh, that's weird."
"Yea, you're telling me. So, those guy earlier, your boyfriend or something."
I wrinkled my nose in disgust, "Uh, no, brothers"
"Oh, that's cool. They seemed to have forgotten you momentarily."
"Yea", I smiled, "Girls seem to do that to them."
"So, have you had a tour of the school yet?"
I shook my head.
"Well, would you like one?"
"Yea, that would be great."
His face lit up. He seemed really nice but his attitude wasn't flirty, it was just very friendly. He showed me the school and the secrets to surviving. I got the down low on the school babies', other cliques, cool tables in the dining room, and my brain was filling with all this trying to remember.
"What school are you transferring from?"
I looked up at this very inquisitive boy.
"I didn't, I was privately tutored. This is my first high school."
"WHAT! Oh my gosh. I have so much to teach you."
I laughed, "Why are you so nice to me?"

He looked puzzled by my question, "Why wouldn't I be nice? You're new and I was the new kids a few years ago, so I know how it feels."

"So, basically, you pity me?"

"No, I want to be friends plus you're like super-hot and all the guys will want to be around you."

I thought his comment was bold but I went with it.

"Where are your other friends? Won't they miss you?" I questioned him back.

It was his turn to laugh this time, "I didn't want to overwhelm you with too much at one time. Sometimes my friends can be....well, they don't think before they talk."

I nodded, "Oh. Well, I believe I am well rounded and can handle a little immaturity."

Bruce laughed, "That's the better word for it."

We walked on and talked more. Bruce was very interesting he is an only child and his parents work at a local store but they don't have a whole lot of money. I felt bad because my family is very wealthy. I didn't really want to say anything about my side of the family but he asked a lot of questions by now he must have figure out my family had money.

"So, what does your family do?"

This is something I didn't want him to ask. I don't want it to get awkward.

"Uh...my father owned a major finance corporation that he sold. No big deal."

Actually, he sold it for a few billion dollars and he invested half and put the other half in a high interest bank. He separated the money and split some of the money into bank accounts for us. Whatever the interest is made off that portion of the money is what we could spend. I've had mine saved up for a while. There wasn't a whole lot I wanted. "Oh, well that's cool."

I shrugged, "Yea." I hated it when people made it a big deal about me having a lot of money.

It was quiet for a few seconds.

"So, did you want to hang out later and meet the gang? I mean if you wanted to. You don't have to. It's not a big deal. I mean it is but it's not."

He rambled on and on.

"Bruce."

"Yes" He finally stopped talking.

"I will have to ask my parents, but I think I would like to hang out."

He smiled a big grin.

"Ok, umm I can give you my number and you can call me to let me know what going on and I'll come get you. Well, I can't drive yet, so my mom will come to get you."

He blushed, embarrassed.

"That sounds fine."

"Coolio!" He got super excited. He seemed like he was going to be fun but there something…off about him. Everyone had their differences and I wasn't going to judge his. We walked down the hall, "Ok. You see Jenny down there. She is wearing the pink skirt that could be her panties. Total grody by the way not something I want to see. I giggled at his vocabulary. *Grody?* "She is a big no-no. She is like the kind of girl who would tell you, you're her best friend and then make you wish you were dead and you would never know she was the one setting you up. The more desperate you become to be popular the worse she makes life for you. Like legit, she almost made this girl commit suicide last year."

"She sounds awful but looks sweet."

"Yea on the outside", Bruce stated, "The inside is pure evil."

Jenny has short blond hair, rosy cheeks, blue eyes, a pound and a half of make-up, slim figure but not much curves, and a sweet smile. I sniffed the air and really expensive hooker perfume. She is rubbing all over this guy who apparently plays football by the letter jacket he has on.

"What about the guy?"

"OH… that's Robert." Bruce stuck his finger in his mouth and made a gagging sound, "I hate to admit but we used to be BFFs."

"What happened?"

"You know people grow apart and start liking different things."

I could sense Bruce's body language and could tell he wasn't being truthful but I wasn't going to push. I of all people know what it's like to have to keep a secret, secret."

"Well his loss anyway."

Bruce looked at me appreciatively and smiled.

Bruce looked down at me, "Are you ok?"

"Yea… Why?"

"Your cheeks are all red and you look like you're getting a little pale."

I felt my head and it wasn't hot. I had a little bit of a headache but nothing to worry about.

"Yea fine, just a little headache."

Bruce smiled but I don't think he believed it was just a headache. I really didn't feel bad.

"Maybe we should cut the tour short so you can sit down for a few."

I nodded and we called it quits. We walked down the hall to my next class and the hallway started to spin. The next thing I know this really big tall guy was catching me as I fell to the ground. His arms were so warm. I felt like I was freezing. I felt so groggy. The lights hurt my eyes as I tried to open them. When I finally came to I realized I was in the nurses' station covered in blankets. I tried to sit up but the nurse caught me.

"No honey, you need to sit back. Rest a few moments, here, drink this it will make you feel better. She handed me a warm cup of tea. I took a sip, "Yuck, this is gross."

She laughed, "Believe me, I know but it helps a lot so drink up."

I took a few more sips and it never got any better.

"What happened?"

"Well, what do you remember?"

I tried to think back but only small bit came to the surface, "Not much, just feeling dizzy and someone catching me. Who was that anyway?"

She looked uncomfortable answering that, "Well, one of the Blackfoot boys."

She didn't seem to want to give me a lot of information.

"Oh ok. Can I go now?"

She nodded, "If you feel like you're up to it."

I thanked her and grabbed my bags. I walked out and the first person I wanted to see was Bruce because he saw firsthand what happened. I looked and couldn't find him anywhere. I walked out of the school and he was sitting with his back against the brick building. As soon as he saw me turn the corner I felt like I was being tackled.

"OMG... babe, what happened?"

"Did you just say OMG?"

He laughed, "Yes."

I looked at him, "Bruce can we go somewhere and talk?"

He looked concerned, "Yea wanna walk to the dinner? It's not far from here."

I nodded. We made our way over and we came in front of this cute woodsy place. It wasn't far from the school. It was wood sided with a green roof. It had cool bear and elf picture hanging inside. All the tables were wooded and looked like someone made them. It had that very cozy cabin feeling. We sat at a table in the corner and Bruce looked at me, "Ok so what's with all the secret stuff?"

"Huh, Oh I need you to tell me who the guy was who caught me and exactly what happened?"

He seemed confused, "This is what you wanted to talk about?"

"Shhh...yes, Please now tell me."

He shrugged, "Fine I mean there isn't a whole lot but you started to walk funny and that tall guy came out of nowhere and as you feel he jumped forward and caught you. Then he ran through the crowd knocking people over to get you to the nurse. Now that you mention it, it is a bit strange."

"Well do you know what he looks like?"

"No way," Bruce's eyes widened, "Turn around and you will see."

"What?" I turned in my seat and looked through the glass window. On the other side of the highway was a very tall

boy about seventeen maybe older. He was built like some
of the other tan boys around here with dark hair and brown
eyes. He was very muscular and had short, brown hair.
"What's he doing here?"
I looked back to Bruce and we both looked back again,
"Well were did he go? We both saw the same thing right?"
I looked at Bruce, "Uh yea I sure hope so."
"Mace, your right, something is awfully weird."
We decided to call our meeting quits and go home for the
day. I hope the school didn't call mom. She will freak. I
waited for Sage at his car and ten minutes after the bell
rang he came around the corner with some girl. Go figure!
She was taller than me (of course) with brown hair, brown
eyes, slender build. She was pretty. She had a small button
nose and cute cheeks. She got dimples when she smiled.
Her eyes caught mine when she got close to the car and she
gave Sage a hurt look. She looked me over and crossed her
arms over her chest noticing I was a bit top heaver that she
was. I could tell she was very insecure. I caught eyes with
Sage.
"It's about time you got here. Who's the lady?" I gave her a
cute smile and she returned an unsure one.
"Elly, this is my sister Macy." He said gesturing to me,
Macy, this is Elly."
She finally gave me a genuine smile now that she knew I
wasn't one of his "others".
"Nice to meet you Elly, now can we go home now?"
He gave me a quit being a pain look. We all got in the car
and made it home. Trying to avoid mom I snuck upstairs. I
got to my room and closed the door. I looked around my
room and I noticed a few things had been moved around. It

wasn't where I left it. I looked to make sure nothing was missing and no money or jewelry was gone must have been my annoying brothers which didn't surprise me. I walked to the door and opened it to be greeted by Tanner, my older brother.

"You scared me."

He pushed past me and walked around my room sniffing like a crazed dog.

"What are you doing?"

He looked at me, "Nothing, did you have someone is here recently? Like a boy maybe."

My jaw dropped, "Are you kidding me? I was going to ask you butts the same question. Some of my stuff was moved and YOU," I poked my finger in his chest, "were one of the only ones here." I accused him.

He huffed and walked out.

"Attitude."

I got my stuff and got ready for bed. I pulled my sheets down and climbed in. I tried to get comfy but there was something in my bed. I reached down under the covers to find out what it is. It was an envelope.

Huh. I opened it up but there was only a blank piece of paper.

Stinkin' brothers.

I closed my eyes and drifted off.

Chapter 3

I was still adjusting to the new town and the new home. I turned the shower nozzle to hot and let the water heat up. I stared into the mirror, as if fogged up. I looked over at the door and made sure I locked it, the last thing I needed was my brothers or sister walking in on me. Fog filled the room as the water heated up. I raised my hands, palm up, to my side and let the heat spread through my body. The fog started to swirl around me and formed a cloud. As I moved my hands the fog moved with them and I pushed the fog together until there was enough condensation for water to drop and I smiled as I made in rain in my bathroom. I giggled to myself. I put my hands in front of me and pushed out and the fog dissipated once again. I curled my fingers in all except for my pointer finger and reached out, twirling my finger around in circles. The water copied my movement, moving in circles. I took my other hand, palm up, starting from the below my hip raising my hand up in the air. The water started to rise, still moving in circles as I created a water tornado. All the water was sucked into the tornado and I flicked my hand and the water tornado stretched until it was over the shower curtain. I flicked my other hand and all water tunneled into the bath tub.

A knock at the door startled me and the water tornado shatters like, and water falls into the tub and floor.
"Hurry up. You're taking forever."
"I just got in", I huffed back.
Quickly I stepped into the shower and bathed. I stepped out and towel dried. I loved playing with my powers but I can't do it often without the fear of getting caught always hanging on my shoulders. I love my family but I hate being so different and having to always hide it. I wrapped the towel around me and walked out. Tanner was standing there rolling his eyes. We have a big house and a lot of bathrooms. This bathroom has a very large walk in shower with multiple shower heads and a large garden tub bottom. So needless to say this is our favorite bathroom in the house. I walk by my brother.
"Ewe clothes"
This time I rolled my eyes as I walked past him and went to my room. I keep all my bathroom stuff in my closet. I opened my bedroom door to reveal my pink room with my pink and black bed spread. My room is huge with a huge walk in closet, with a smaller walk in closet I keep all my bathroom stuff in. I grabbed my hair dryer and stood in front of my body sized mirror. I grabbed my round brush and begin to blow dry my long hair, it takes forever.
Finally, after forever, my hair is dry. I straighten it and throw on my pink, black, and red leggings. I look through my closet and find my long, red shirt pulling my long hair out and letting it fall down my back. I slipped on my red flats and walked out my bedroom door.
"Hey Abby what's going on?" I asked my sister as I entered the kitchen.

"I just found the coolest apartment just down the road from college. It's not what I'm used to being in the woods and all. A little secluded but it's big enough and offers what I want."

"That's cool, when can we see it?"

She tilted her head, thinking.

"Maybe today, tomorrow, maybe never." She smiled. I smirked at her and she winked. I have always looked up to my big sister. So her getting out on her own and not living at home anymore was going to be weird. Even though our ages are so far apart, we were actually pretty close being the only girls.

"Well, we can go now. The guy who is showing the apartments said he will be there in about an hour."

I squealed and jumped up and down. We grabbed our jackets and went to the door.

"Oh I forgot my phone. I'll meet you in the car." I hurried and ran up the stairs to my room. I looked around and saw it was sitting in the nook by the window. I ran over to get it and something moved out of the corner of my eye. I glanced up as I grabbed the phone. I had to double take and I felt my stomach drop for a second. I looked again and I could have sworn I saw something. A part of my pixie gift is photographic memory but I didn't get to see, whatever it was, long enough to get a good picture. I put my hands on the nook and leaned into the window, trying really hard to look. I could see all the leaves and bugs crawling on the ground. As I age, my senses heighten. My vision is amazing, if I concentrate. Otherwise it's mostly normal, I have to almost "zoom" in.

I looked out the window but couldn't see anything. The horn honked and I had to rush away from the window but that image was still stuck in my head. I racked my brain but couldn't get a clear image of what I saw. I let it go for now, but I have that feeling, that we aren't as alone as I thought.

Chapter 4

"OH MY GOODNESS...this is so cute. It looks way bigger on the inside than on the outside."
"Yea, Abby this is really cute."
Abby smiled, "Wait till you see the master bedroom. There is a huge window in there."
I jumped, excited. We ran down the hall to a large doorway Abby and mom not far behind me. I opened the door and walked in. It was so open and pretty it took my breath away. The walls were earth tone colors. Light brown but darker than tan, the floor was all hardwood, and the windows were double windows. I opened the windows; they opened like double doors, opening from the inside out. I stood there staring out the window. My hair picked up and blew behind me as the wind blew into the window.
"It's just so open...."
I could hear my family talking behind me but I was so zoned out into the window I wasn't hearing them anymore. I breathed in the air and as I did all these new scents hit my nose. I could smell the musk of deer miles away, I could smell the neighbors cooking and anything that came with the breeze. I turned around and smelled and I smelled like lilac and chocolate something. I smelled again and followed the scent till my nose was on my sister's face.
"What...are...you...doing?"
I opened my eyes and was shocked to find she was the scent. I walked to my mom and smelled her. She was a hint

of chocolate and strawberry. I didn't understand why they smelled like this or why I just now smell it.

I must be getting something new. I knew something about my smell was different the other day but it wasn't this much of a difference.

"Do we stink or something?"

I looked at my mom, "Uh he-he well, you see. I thought I smelled something funny." I said shrugging.

They both looked at me then each other.

"Ok..."

I blushed and walked back to the window. I looked out and took a big whiff. It was amazing all the different smells. I could hear the wind rippling through the trees heading towards me. I leaned out the window letting the breeze flow past my cheeks. My nose wrinkled as a very musky smell hit my nose. It was a foul musk, like a dead animal smell. I peered out and I could hear dogs growling. I focused my eyes and could see what looked like, wolves. From how big they were from this far away, they must be massive up close. I looked back to see my mom and sister looking the house over not even aware of the danger a few miles away. I looked back, surprise taking over my face. The giant wolves were just...gone. I looked as hard as I could but couldn't see any wolves. I knew as big as they were it would be really hard to hide.

"Are you gonna just enjoy my yard or what?"

I jumped, "Uh yea, I mean no."

"Are you ok? You have been actin funny ever since we got here?"

I gave a convincing smile, "Uh, yea. I'm fine; I'm just trying to take everything in. I mean, you're gonna be gone now, at your own house. It's just exciting."

Abby smiled and rolled her eyes, obviously not believing my story.

"OK. Whatever."

I glanced back at the window again before following Abby around the corner into the kitchen. I didn't see anything after that but the smell was something I had never smelled before. I was going to remember that for a while.

"Yea, I know right. These cabinets are the perfect color. They go great with the maple hardwood floors. It's amazing whoever built this apartment really put a lot of thought into it."

My mom nodded in agreement, "Yes, they did a great job. The walls are perfect. The light brown walls go great with the floor as well. They put a lot of thought into decoration as well."

They were nodding back and forth complimenting this and that. I really didn't get all this matching this and oh that so goes with that. Yea, I'm so over it. I just really wanted to see what her place looks like and how far away she would be living from me. Actually, it's not that far. It's like 25 miles from here and mostly main highway. Towards the end its back roads and that takes the longest. For the most part though, it's fairly easy to get here. What I like the most is we are surrounded by woods. Here, the woods are few and far between. That's how I think I was able to see those wolves. I wonder if they are seen a lot around here. I don't want to ask too many questions. People might try to hunt them. I just wonder what made them that big or how they have been hiding. I mean, they were huge.

"Wanna go outside?"

I looked up at Abby not seeing she was standing right in front of me for the moments I was thinking. From the look on her face, she apparently had asked me before and has been waiting for my answer. I gave a sweet smile, "Yea, let's do that."
"Ok, whatever."
She turned and she and mom walked out of the front door and I followed them out.
"This is where the garage will go and over there, the storage building to keep all the extra crap I know I will bring home. Also, I'm thinking about getting a dog to ward off the other animals and strangers. There has been some weird talk around here about men roaming the woods." She huffed in annoyance.
"Men?" I asked her and she looked at me with a smirk.
"Just your kind Mace...creepy."
I rolled my eyes and kept walking out. I looked towards the woods where I saw the wolves. I wanted to go over there but I feared Abby and mom would follow me and see evidence of the wolves. So I reluctantly hung around and listened to Abby talk about her boring plans that are going to take years for her to do. Unless she gets a boyfriend and let's face it...she is way to mean.
"We are going back in, you coming?" mom stopped and asked me as they turned to head back to the house.

I shook my head, "Nah, Im'a hang out here for a little while."
She smiled and turned still listening to Abby's rambling.

I was waiting till they were inside and walked over towards the woods. My insides were shaking at the thought of actually coming face to face with those giants. My spine tingled at the thought. I came to the edge of the woods and stepped in. I smelled and it smelled of rotten flesh with another smell totally different, like raspberries or something. What a heck of a combination. I stepped again but felt like I have entered through an invisible force field. I felt like I had walked though maybe a water fall that wasn't wet, that's the only way I can describe it and it make any since but even that didn't make much since. I shrugged it off and kept walking towards the smell. The closer I got to where the wolves were fighting, the stronger the smell got. I replayed the image of them in my head over. I walked over to a tree that one of the wolves rubbed against, putting my nose up to the tree and sniffed. That one smelled like the raspberries. I went to the other tree the other wolf hit as they rolled around fighting. I sniffed but drew back fast. That wolf seriously needed a bath. His fur was all dirty looking and he smelled way worse than he looked. I turned to walk back and stepped in a hole, almost tripping. I stopped and looked down. It was a huge print. It had to be a foot long. I bent down to touch it rubbing my hands across it when that terrible stench hit my nose. My nose wrinkled. A twig snapped and I looked up to big yellow, empty eyes. The only thought I had was... I was going to die.

Chapter 5

      That smell was overwhelming and those eyes belong to the devil. He growled low and deep, my stomach sunk. He stepped forward and the sun hit his fur. It was a muddy brown and black. He was the ugliest thing I had ever seen. He was so large, his head was the size of...of...a really big head. His teeth were brown and wet with blood and drool and had to be at least 3-4 inches long. Imagine that going through your skin. He growled, showing his teeth, meaning he meant business. He looked as long as a car and as tall as a bus. I should have been more afraid and I didn't understand why I wasn't. I felt like I was shaking so hard the tree next to me would lose its leaves. He raised his muzzle and sniffed the air. He looked almost surprised at whatever he found and he kept eyeing me but didn't attack yet. It was like he was afraid to see what would happen....or he was teasing me. I wasn't sure which one. What am I saying, he is an animal. All he knows is to eat, sleep, and protect him or herself. He sniffed again but stepped closer to me. I didn't move still not sure what's the best move to make. He growled again and bent low, readying himself to pounce. I knew I had to move fast or be wolf meat. He lepta out from behind the bush and I took off in the other direction going deeper into the woods. I was afraid I was falling into his trap, maybe this is what he wanted to happen. Now I would be alone and it would be too late by the time my mom could find me. This was way better when I watched it on animal planet. I felt heat on the back of my neck I was too afraid to turn around because I knew he was playing with me. He could have easily caught me by now. He was letting me get further into the woods. I had to do something now. Without further thought, I jumped and grabbed a limb pulling myself up. The wolf jumped and tried to grab my leg barley missing. I looked down at the snarling wolf. He was obviously mad because he was out smarted. He jumped up clawing at the tree. I raised my feet to escape his sharp claws. Every time he jumped he got a little closer to me. I looked up to get further into the tree but all of the limbs were out of my reach. The wolf was so large the tree would shake and the limbs would tremble. I felt it giving way. I panicked and the wolf saw this. He jumped scratching the bottom of my leg. I felt the warm trickle of blood dripping down my leg. I could smell it and it gaged me. The limb cracked and I felt my body falling to the ground. Right before I hit, I felt this enormous power fill my veins and everything went black.

"Macy......Macy, Are you ok."
"She must have fallen from the tree I found her under."
There was a man's voice but I didn't recognize it.
"Thank you so much for finding her. I don't know what would have happened to her if you hadn't."
"It's no problem ma'am. I'm just glad I found her when I did. She looks like she took a hard hit"
I stirred a little, "Uhhhhh"
"Macy! You're alive, thank goodness."
I could hear his footsteps and the man walked away. I sniffed the air but all I could smell was my own overbearing scent of blood. I opened my eyes and squinted at the bright light.

"Honey, what were you thinking running off like that? You were all the way on the neighbors land."

"Uggg...I was just walking..."

"Walking...you were nine miles into the woods. That man's house is like twenty minutes away."

I looked at my mom and sister, "What? I didn't go that far. I don't know how I got down there and who was that man?"

"He is the neighbor and wasn't very happy about you trespassing but because he found you passed out, he is overlooking it. This is serious. Did you see anyone or hear anything?"

"No...NO. Just a big dog and it scared me."

"Did he bite you, is this where you got those scratches?"

"MOM, seriously," Abby cut in, "Do you know how big that dog would have had to have been to make a cut that big. Macy is just a dork and got really lost running from a dog that probably wasn't even after her."

Mom huffed, "Do you need to go to the hospital? Is anything broken?"

"Mom, NO. I am fine." I think

I leaned up and winced as I moved my leg. I looked down at my bandaged leg...blood leaking through the bandage.

"Here, Mr. Hottie Indian man said to put this on your leg after you get out of the shower and before bed."

I looked up at Abby, "Mr. Hottie Indian man?"

"Yea, the guy that saved you. He had like long black hair and the body of an Olympian goddess."

I laughed but winced at the pain, "So did this hottie Indian guy give a name?"

Abby shrugged, "If he did, I wouldn't have heard it I was too busy checking out his muscles."

"Anyway girls, I think Macy needs to rest. Let's get out of here."

We all nodded and walked back to the car. I gave the forest one last glance as we drove away.

"Macy, come on were gonna be late."

I huffed at my impatient brother who keeps rushing me out of the shower. I get in and not five seconds I'm already being rushed out. My leg only aches now and has healed surprisingly well to how deep those cuts were. Good thing that man bandaged me up, if my mom had actually seen the wound, I don't know what she would have freaked out more over...the wound our how fast I heal. I only got the cut a few days ago and the stitches they put in have already came out and the cut has mostly healed. There won't be a scar, if there is you will barely be able to see it. My mom was very reluctant to let me go to school today, but I finally talked her into it. My brothers thought it was freaking hilarious that I fell. Tanner, however, has been acting rather strange. He saw my cuts by accident and freaked out at how bad they looked and he, somehow, knew that it wasn't caused by the tree and wanted to know exactly how I got them and when. I told him it wasn't a big deal but then mom had to bring up I said something about a dog and now he refuses to let me go anywhere by myself. He says, the dogs might still be out there and remember me. I think there is something he isn't telling me about these dogs and now he keeps trying to look at my leg. Which, I can't let him see because it's almost healed now. He is already asking too many questions and that would only make things worse.

"Macy, are you ok?"

Tanner's voice came through the door.

"Yes, Tanner I'm just taking a shower."

"Do you feel weird at all?"

"Tanner, can I please take a shower in peace?"

       I was standing there, letting the hot water run over me. I lifted my leg and looked down. The scratches were barely visible. I ran my fingers down my leg, tracing the claw marks. They had to have been six inches or longer. After the bathroom felt like a sauna I finally turned the water off. I got out and got dressed. I had my skinny jeans, bright pink tank, and pink flats. I through in some accent jewelry to change it up. I blow dried my long hair and straightened it. I added a few dabs of makeup some eye shadow, eye liner, and a little mascara. Finally, I was walking out the door and guess that was standing outside the door.

"Tanner, I'm fine."

He sighed and leaned his head back against the wall.

"You just don't understand.

I looked at Tanner, "Please, telling me you're kidding? It's just a scratch and what would I not understand?"

He laughed," I mean imagine if you could be like the wolverine or something. Look, your ears are already getting pointy." He grabbed my pointy pixie ears and I smacked his hand away. My ears have always been a problem for me because they are very pointy and my family just considered it a small birth defect. No one knows there is actually a reason, no matter how bad I wish I could have someone to confide in.

 "I'm just not going to respond to that" I walked passed him and went towards the door. I smelled mom cooking pancakes.

"Mmm, mom whatever you making smells great."

She smiled at me but it was that 'I'm really worried about you face.'

"Mom, I am fine and please don't tell me Tanner has been talking to you about werewolf because there is no such thing."

She laughed, "No, I'm just worried about you. I mean, you were miles away from where you said you were, blacked out, and a man was taking care of you. I mean, who knew what could have happened to you."

"Mom, I am fine. I promise."

She sighed, giving in. I grabbed a few pancakes and headed to school; Tanner not far behind me.

We made it to school and we got out of the car. It was a very intense care ride. No one really spoke. It was really strange. Someone knows something and they are having a lot of trouble not telling me. We walked into the tall brick building and a million scents hit my nose at the same time. I put my hand over my nose. Tanner looked back and Sage smelled himself.

"Do I smell that bad?" Tanner and sage looked at each other and shrugged. It was almost too much to stand. There were millions of different scents swirling around from lemons to rotten cheese. BLAH! I just had to grin and bear it. I walked around corner and Bruce was standing in the hallway. He glanced my way as I walked in and gave me a big welcoming smile. As I got closer I caught a hint of blue berry, what a relief.

"Well, look what the dog dragged in."

I stopped, "What?"

His smiled dropped to an embarrassed one. "Oh, it's just a saying. I'm not a big cat person."

I laughed, "Oh. I thought. Never mind. So what's been going on?"

"Oh nothing, just been hanging. I haven't seen you in a few days, Where you been hiding?"

I shrugged, "Ya know. Just doing what girls do. I have been here, you just haven't seen me."

He nodded but didn't say much. He seemed to be bothered by something.

"Bruce, what's wrong."

He looked at me but then looked away quickly.

"I just wanted to ask you something but I didn't know how you would react?"

"Well, you will never know unless you ask."

He chuckled a little and it was the cutest chuckle I couldn't help but smile along with him.

I thought he was very charming but I couldn't do a relationship right now. I mean what if I got to close and they found out about me and freaked out. I was calm on the outside but freaking out on the inside.

"I really like you Macy, a lot; you are fun, and sweet."

"Uh, you are really nice to Bruce, but...."

"Please, let me finish." I nodded and Bruce continued, "Ok, so would you still want to be friends with me even if you knew I.....was gay."

"Oh thank gosh."

He laughed, "What?"

"I thought you were gonna ask me out."

His jaw dropped, "I am not that bad. OMG, do you find me that unattractive?"

I stared at him and busted out laughing. In between my laughs I said, "Did you really just say OMG, and no I'm just not ready to be in a relationship and I was freaking out because I really like hanging out with you these past few weeks and I didn't want to ruin it."

"Well, sorry but I don't swing that way." He smirked and now I was so embarrassed.

"So, you're really gay?"

He looked at me and gave me this "duh what are you talking about look"

"Uh yea, have been as long as I can remember it's hard to find guy friends and then you know, you tell them and all the sudden you're a freak."

He had no idea but I was a freak all the time. I wished so bad I could tell him my secret. I looked up to him and smiled letting him know I was listening. We walked down the hallway. He was in mid-sentence and as if right on Que, a football hit Bruce in the back of the head. He fell to his knees and I looked back to see a few boys from the football team his "use to be friends."

"Hey faggot, found you a new friend, huh? If I were you, girly, I'd find better friends. I could give you something he couldn't. I nice big...."

"Choose your next words wisely."

We both turned to see the really tall, tan boy from my first day of school, the one who gave me the eerie creeps.

"What are you gonna do about it, huh? You gonna take all of us?" He said as he motioned to all his friends around him.

He boy smiled, "No" He got into the boy's face, towering over him by at least a foot and a half and all his would be friends backed up.

"Just you," he smirked.

Even his smirk was menacing.

"Drake, man, back off," The boy, Drake, smirked back and pretended to turn before throwing a punch, easily caught by the mysterious boy. The larger boy squeezed and twisted Drakes hand as if he was a rag doll. Using little effort, he stepped closer forcing Drake to sink to the floor. I almost thought I heard him growl but that wouldn't make any since. I helped Bruce up and felt behind his head to make sure there wasn't a bump. I looked back to the boy and he stared at me almost like, waiting for me to say something. He looked back at Drake and whispered something in his ear, making Drake's face turned pale white. He nodded and the boy released his hand.

Our eyes connected one last time before he was gone once again. I still never got his name. Ill guess I'll call him Mr. Mysterious because everything about him is a mystery.

Drake stood and walked off without saying a word.

Bruce looked at me, "What the heck, just happened?" I shrugged unable to speak. Those eyes looked so strange.

"Bruce, did you see his eyes."

Bruce looked at me, "Eyes? Did you see his abs?

I smacked Bruce and rolled my eyes.

"What, just saying."

"No, I mean I swear they were like brown, solid black, and then changed back to brown."

"Whatever, his eyes ain't what I was looking at."

I laughed.

Those eyes would stick with me for days after that. We haven't had another incident with Drake or his friends. I don't know what Mr. Mysterious said but they have steered clear of us ever since. If we even come in the same room as him, he leaves instantly. I don't hear any complaining though. Bruce and I have become even better friends. Ever since he got his secret off his chest he is more himself and people are starting to notice his change. He seems not to care. Which, I don't think he should change himself to make everyone else happy.

Bruce sat down next to me at the lunch table with some of our other friends.

"So, I asked my mom and she was totally cool with it, if you wanted to have a sleep over at my house?"

"I'll ask my mom but that would be cool."

He looked up and everyone nodded.

From left to right you have Eric ad Eli the twins. They have red hair, blue eyes and average bodies. Ashley our fashion adviser, always keeping up with the latest trend, she can be a little out there. She has brown hair, brown eyes, about 5'6 she was average but pretty.

Next, we have Amber and Chase. They are the couple always sucking their faces off. Amber is pretty, 5'5 slim, blond, with blue eyes. Chase is average 5'11 slight build, blond, blue eyes. If they weren't dating I would swear they were brother and sister. It's kind of creepy.

There was a lot a chaos across the lunch room and I see my brothers Sage and Tanner making a scene. All I heard was something about Tanner stole Sages French fries.

I have actually gotten this scent thing almost under control or I'm getting more used to it. The only time it gets bad is if a really bad smell drifts through. I could smell every food and body odor. Mix that in with the scents and my nose is so confused I just ignore it. I don't know how to separate the smells. I even catch a strange wet dog smell every now and then.

The rest of the day went by without incident. I just had to ask my mom about the sleep over.

School was finally over and Tanner and I headed back to the car. As I was walking I started to feel a little dizzy but it came and went. I looked out of the window and I could see all the colors of the trees and plants so clear as if we weren't going sixty down the highway. I rubbed my neck, I felt like I was getting a headache. I squeezed my eyes shut hoping the feeling would go away but when I opened my eyes it was worse. All the colors were starting to blend together and my vision got blurry. I felt my insides tingle and all these colors started to appear surrounding everything. I grabbed Tanners arm and he looked at me.

"What's the matter?"

Everyone looked at me but I couldn't say anything.

"Macy, what's wrong?"

I couldn't figure out where the colors were coming from or why I was seeing them. A pain shot through my head and I screamed. My brother swerved almost crashing as I held my head with one hand and squeezed his arm with the other.

"Macy!!!!"

I could hear their voices yelling but I couldn't answer and slowly their voices drifted away.

Chapter 6

It was bright, very bright. There were lights everywhere and the voices were all around me. I couldn't make out what they were saying. All I could see were....colors, lots of colors. There were blues, greens, yellow, reds, and purples. There were more colors some mixed but I couldn't figure out where they were coming from.

"Her eyes are open!"

I heard a man but I didn't recognize his voice.

"Macy, can you hear me?"

I looked towards the voice and all around this man was a bright blue lining.

"Am I dead?" I hardly recognized my own voice.

"No dear. You are not dead; you had a severe panic attack. You will make a full recovery."

I looked towards where the voice was coming from but all I could see were the blues and greens. It didn't make any since. How could I have had a panic attack?

I was sitting up in the bed, eating some soup my mom brought me.

"This is the second time she has blacked out. Don't you think it could be more serious than a simple panic attack?"

"Ma'am, we ran tests and everything was normal. I assure you, your daughter is perfectly fine. I just need to ask her a few questions, and then you can go in and see her."

I could see the frustration in my mom's face. Her scent was distraught, so it matched her mood. I looked back at mom and the doctor. I didn't think they knew I could hear them but with my enhanced hearing, I can hear every word loud and clear. Something is different though, all there colors I'm seeing are something that has never happened before and I don't know how to explain it. It's like there is this coloring around each person, kind of like they each have different scents. Now, they have scents and different colors like their aurora. I don't know what any of this means. All these new changes were overwhelming for me. I didn't know how to control the scents or find out who they went to. I just wanted things to go back to normal. I don't understand why I was born like this, with these gifts, and never able to use them or tell anyone. The doctor came in and his scent hit me as soon as the door opened. I wrinkled my nose, he smelled like a wet dog and a hint of cinnamon.

"Is everything ok, Miss. Ryan?"
I looked up at his smiling face. He had dark hair, dark skin, blue eyes, and was really tall. He had a 5 o' clock shadow working its way in and he seemed really nice. He had this weird vibe coming off of him. Like, it made part of me wants to bow down and do everything he commanded but the other part wasn't affected at all. He had a bright greenish, blue tint light around his skin. It would glow bright and then go dim. I didn't know if I controlled that or if he did. Was this something new? I looked all over his body looking at the colors mixing together. He cleared his throat causing my face to snap to his.

"My name is Dr. Vaughn, I needed to ask you a few questions if that's alright. You know you didn't strike me as the flirtatious type." He smirked.

I blushed. I didn't realize it looked like I was checking him out but didn't know what to say now.

"Anyway, how many times do you think you have these episodes of blacking out?"

I looked him in the eyes this time; I didn't want to give him another boost to his ego.

"I only had it happen one other time. They don't happen that often." He nodded.

I wanted to close my nose or get a candle. Did he have a pet in here?

I couldn't get that smell out of my nose that wet dog smell. I didn't know what kind of scent this would be for a person.

"Look, on this paper are some symptoms. Have you had any of these before your episodes?"

I looked down at the paper and went over them.

Light headed
Blurred Vision, Seeing spots
Weakness
Sensations the room is moving
Ringing in the ears
Dizziness
Fatigue
Sweating
Nausea

Paleness
Headache

I looked back up meeting his eyes. After a few minutes, I
could feel a flustered vibe. I knew it wasn't me so it had to
be Dr. Vaughn. I didn't understand why he would be upset
or over what.
Well, I've had a few of these like the room moving and
paleness but that's it... The only thing I remember is
blackness taking over and then waking up." I answered
him.
He looked at me and rubbed the back of his neck. When he
talked, he looked at my face but I would meet his eyes and
he would divert them. I kept getting the feeling he either
didn't want me to look in his or he didn't want to look in
mine. Well, where I grew up when you spoke to someone,
you had to look them in the eyes. If you didn't you were
disrespecting them. He seemed to have an opposite effect.
"Are you sure that's all that happened?"
He looked at me like he knew I wasn't telling the truth. It's
not like I could tell him, oh by the way, I'm a pixie and I'm
seeing this green glow around you but it only started when
I passed out and woke back up.
"Umm... yes, that's it." He nodded, "Um, Dr. Vaughn, did
you have a dog in here? It smells like wet dog."
He seems a little taken aback from what I said and looked
through my chart, "What are you looking for?"

He never answered me and he even completely ignored my
question.

"So you didn't have any of the other symptoms listed. Its ok, I'm just making sure. Its normal for people to feel embarrassed about something or afraid we may not understand."

He looked at me with a very sincere look as he spoke the last part. Like that last sentence had a double meaning. I could feel my heart going a hundred miles a second.
"I said that's it, that's all I remember."
"Ok" He nodded. He looked down at his paper and I fiddled with my hands. I interlaced my fingers and I started to feel this tingling sensation. My palms started to itch. I rubbed my hands together and I saw something drip under my hands. I opened my hands and looked down but didn't see anything. I glanced up and the Dr. was still looking at his paper. I waited till he got up and walked out of the room. I rubbed my hand together and the same thing happened again. It was like very tiny golden sparkles but when I opened my hand they disappeared. I closed my hand and rubbed my thumb to my fingers and I could see the sparkles dropping. My eyes grew big as a pair of saucers and the Dr.'s voice broke my train of thought.
"Are you ok?"
I looked up and he stood in the doorway. "Huh...Oh yea, I'm fine."
He didn't say anything else; he just marked his paper and closed the door. He walked up to my mom and they talked.

I would have listened but I was too busy freaking out over my sparkling dust.

I was looking at my hands and I felt this very dark presents around me. I felt like the room was caving in trying to crush me. The stench hit my nose as soon as I looked up. My eyes stopped when they met a pair of very dark ones. The glow around this man was not green like the doctors. His was dark brown and black. I knew this man was bad news, I didn't know how, but I knew. He stepped to the door to my room and cracked it open. As soon as he did his stench hit the room more powerful that I had smelt before. It was that same foul smelling scent as when I was at my sister's house when those wolves were fighting. I felt my heart pick up its pace and I began to panic. My heart monitor went sky high and all these alarms began to sound and blink. He wasn't even fazed by them. He reached inside the door frame and his hands were hideous with long claws. Everyone walked by as if he wasn't even there. I was about to freak out when the doctor looked at me and my panicked eyes met his. He rushed towards the door and the dark man took off down the hall and then just disappeared. The doctor went to touch the door knob and stopped. He looked like he was sniffing the air. He looked at me and walked in slamming the door before anyone else could follow him. He locked it behind him and all the nurses and staff tried the door knob. The doctor spoke fast and rushed. "You could see him?"

I felt like crying I didn't know what was going on.

"I asked could you SEE HIM!" He raised his voice a little at the end and I jumped at his tone but I was too scared to answer.

"I don't understand how you can avoid my commands?"
His voice barely above a whisper without my hearing I
would have never heard him.
"What was he, those claws...?"
His head snapped to mine and he nodded and left the room,
never answering me.

We were walking out of the hospital and my mom
was stuck to my side. She tried talking to me on the way
home but I was so distraught with the whole sparkle and
the creepy man, I could hardly keep my attention to her
questions.
"Honey, are you sure you're ok? Do we need to go back to
the doctors?"
I looked at her and forced a smiled, "Ma, I am fine, I
promise. I'm just.... really tired."
My mom opened the door and we walked in to the house.
All my brothers starred at me but didn't really say anything.
They all gave me a reassuring smile as I walked past them.
However, that wasn't very reassuring. I expected everyone
to run and hug me but no one moved. They just all stared at
me. I walked down the hall to my room. My walls were all
pink and my bed was pink but it had black flowers all over
it. My room was pretty big with a really large walk-in
closet and bathroom. I sat in my room for a little while until
I heard voices outside my door. I focused in and them
instead of hearing who they were I could sense them. Their
scents hit me first, it was cinnamon and cherry. I didn't
know who the scents matched up to but I could feel their
presents. Now I listened and I could tell it was dad and
Sage. I got up and walked closer to the door.

"There was something that doctor didn't tell us but I couldn't figure it out. I mean did you see the way she looked in the hospital. I thought she was going to die. Then her body did that weird thing and...I just don't know what to think. I mean, do you think it's possible.
Your sister is not some kind of freak. There is a perfectly good explanation, the doctor just didn't tell me. I'll talk to your mom and see if she knows anything, her and that doctor spoke for a really long time."
Do they know about me and what did happen in that hospital?

Knock knock

"Yes Tanner."
Tanner opened the door and he looked terrible. Tanner was the only one in the family other than me who had a different color eyes as mom and dad. It's just weird because blue eyes are dominate and for us to have them it strange.
"Mace, I don't know what to say or how because I know how it's going to sound. You...um, you need to leave, disappear somewhere, anywhere, anywhere but here, before it's too late."
I didn't know what to say but my face must have been enough. Tanner sighed, "I know how this sounds but I'm leaving to. We don't belong here with humans."

My eyes widened, "Hu..., you mean you?"
Tanner nodded, "I won't ask you, if you don't ask me. The less we know about each other's differences the better."

Maybe it's about time I leave and find out more about me and who I am. I felt terrified but what if something had happened and I hurt someone. I needed answers to what's going on. I nodded to Tanner and tears fell from my face. I tried to hold them in but it hurts so much leaving all I knew. I walked to my closet and grabbed my bag. I stuffed all the clothes I could, including my rain coat and a blanket. I didn't know how long it would be before I found a more permanent place to stay. Good thing I took girl scouts as a younger girl so if I get stuck in the woods I can make it on my own for a few days. I packed everything and put it by my window; I hardly doubt mom and dad would let me leave after today.

"Tanner, what if something happens? What if…"

"No what ifs," Tanner interrupted me, "Go and I will make sure you get out without notice. Just leave a note or something so everyone doesn't freak out." He laughed like that wasn't going to happen.

I couldn't explain what I felt. My chest felt like it was going to explode with the pain I felt. I looked at Tanner and couldn't help but wonder why he was different and when he started finding out. I had someone here the whole time that knew exactly how I felt and never knew it. It doesn't make any difference now that we are both leaving. He doesn't look like much of a pixie.

I walked over to my desk and grabbed a piece of paper. Everything was about to change and I didn't know for better or worse.

Mom and Dad,

I need to figure out who I am. There are answers I need that you can't give me. Don't worry I will be fine and will be in touch soon.

Love,

Macy

Tanner read over my shoulder and I heard him sigh. His breath hit my neck and his scent of black berry reached my nose. I savored the scent not knowing when I would ever smell it again.

"Mace, you know once you leave and find whatever kind you need, you can never come back. Not here and any contact will have to be very short and in secret."
I looked at Tanner, "What do you know that I don't?"
He looked like he didn't want me to know but he would have to give me some kind of answer or I would find out myself and I think he knew that.
"Let's just say that thing at the hospital you saw, that wasn't his first visit. He has come to see me to and he is getting boulder showing up in the middle of the day in front of that Alpha."
"Alpha what's that?"
"Macy please, we don't have time. You need to go before it gets to dark."

I nodded and grabbed my back pack. I hugged my brother harder than ever before and I could smell the salty tears and he let them fall freely.

"I love you Mace and that's why I am doing this. I will leave a few weeks after you so not to gain suspicion from anyone."

I had a feeling he wasn't just talking about our family.

I left the note on the freshly made bed and I gave one last look to my brother before jumping out the window. I glided through the air looking down at the ground. I used my hands and rubbed my fingers and thumb together creating my sparkling dust throwing it under me. As I went through the dust I slowed and hit the ground lightly.

"Well, that's good to know."

I really didn't know what would happen but it was worth a shot. I looked ahead into the dark woods and took off. I didn't know where it would lead me or what my fate would be now that I am off on my own. I stopped right at the edge of the woods and turned around to look at my house for one last look. My life would never again be the same. Then I stepped into a whole new world, I just didn't know it yet.

Chapter 7

It has been a week since I left but I couldn't help but miss home. I have been staying at a campsite since I left. I walked for days only stopping to sleep or eat. I picked berries or set traps for rabbits and other small animals. I never really encountered any wolves or dangerous animals. I heard them and it gave me chills, hearing that piercing howl in the middle of the night. They woke me a few times in the night, I could hear them growling, running, and fighting back in forth but I never saw any in person. Finally the sun rose and I packed up my gear and any nonperishable food I could carry with me, which wasn't much. I stood and looked around. I wish I knew where to go or which direction I needed to take to find what I am looking for. When I do find someone how do I know I can trust them? Those words that lady told me at the beach never left my mind. She knew what I was, it was part of our gift, and we are an endangered species and hunted for multiple uses.

It was part of our gift, she knew what I was.

If she knew what I was, that meant maybe I could find other people like me, but I had no clue how. I wouldn't even know where to start. I picked up my bowl and started snacking on my berries. First, I need to find a person who is 'different' like me, maybe not my exact species, but a non-human. I had to find answers. I was so aggravated because I felt like there was so much I could do but I had no clue how to do it. I was eating a berry and bit onto something hard.

"Ow. What the..."

I pulled whatever it was and looked at it.

"A seed?"

I dropped it onto the ground and playfully sprinkled my dust on it just to see what would happen. I waited and nothing.

"Oh well, I don't have a green thumb." I kind of giggled to myself.

SNAP

I jumped at the sound of a snapping branch.

Fear crept up in my stomach and I searched the dark forest but to no avail. My eyes have adjusted to the dark but my vision in the darkness wasn't much better than the average human.

I listened and smelled waiting for something to disturb my senses. All the sudden this terrible stench hit my nose and the image of the man at the hospital shot into my mind. I knew I was in trouble and had to get out fast. I grabbed my bag and stuffed anything I could as fast as I could. Food, blankets, and anything else I could grab. I didn't even zip it I just took off running in the opposite direction the stench was coming from. I could feel my heart beating in my chest. I thought my heart was going to explode. Even though I ran with everything I had I can feel his evil presents and his stench closing in on me. I saw a log up ahead and I jump trying to leap over the log but failed. I turned only to be met face to face with what looked like a half human half wolf man. He smelled of dead flesh. His skin was a pale mud brown with patches of fur. He must have been seven feet tall with huge fangs, dripping with drool. I was terrified.

"W...what are you?"

The creature smiled an evil smile. I had to try holding my breath because his stench was almost unbearable. He stepped towards me showing his teeth. I looked for a way out but I couldn't see a way no matter which way I went, my only option was to fight. Before I could even think he leapt at me claws extended, fangs out, he collided with me. I felt like I had been hit by a truck my vision blurred and the breath was knocked out of me. He nudged at me with his nose and pushed me around. He licked my skin when I pushed him away he growled and I pushed on his chin keeping his teeth away from me and his drool dripped down my arm. I rubbed my fingers together and threw dust in his face. He jumped away from me wiping his face. The monster staggered and looked around. He seemed very confused and reached out grabbed objects that weren't there. He became very frightened and ran off through the woods crashing into trees and breaking branches off causing quite a ruckus. I stood and ran as fast as I could the other direction. Even though I was terrified I didn't feel the same way I did at the hospital. This creature seemed different less violent I guess.

I stopped running I thought was far enough away. I breathed shakily. I was completely shaken up, and I tried to stand but now that the adrenaline has somewhat warn off I felt like my legs were Jell-O. I knew I had to get out of here before another one of those, those things or something worse came to investigate the noise. I tried to gather myself together. I looked down and I was covered in mucky, disgusting drool. I sniffed and it was terrible. I couldn't get this smell off of me. I ran through the woods but that stench wouldn't leave my clothes. I was going to have to wash these clothes or get rid of them one. After walking for a few hours my legs were getting weak.

"Hey, is that a...stream."

I could hear the water flowing. I walked a little while longer and finally saw a stream. I looked around and listened but didn't hear anything. I took my clothes off and waded into the water, trying hard to wash the smell from my skin. I changed and washed my clothes but the stench would not leave my skin. I sat there thinking about that monster. He was so ugly and hideous and his skin was nasty looking. Ugggg...

I looked down at my hands; I wonder what the dust did to him. I replayed the action in my head and he was grabbing at imaginary objects. He freaked out and the look of its face was pure terror. What did he see? What did the dust do to him? So technically since I'm a pixie does it make this dust 'pixie dust'? I laughed at the thought of pixie dust. Thinking about Tinker bell, but wasn't she a fairy.

I shrugged my shoulders and rubbed the back of my neck with the cold water. I was still shaken from what had happened. Maybe there is more to this world than I ever knew.

I dipped my hands into the stream and splashed the water into my face. The cold felt good on my tired skin. I reached back down into the stream, all the color drained from my skin as my eyes saw my reflection.

"AHHHHHHHHH" I screamed as I was tackled to the ground so hard my vision blurred and the dark figure stood over me as I blacked out.

"Uuhhhh" I held my head. I reached up to feel my head to make sure I wasn't bleeding or dead one. I reached up but my arm was stopped short. I looked up, "Ow"

My head was throbbing. I looked and I was chained. My heart sped up and I grabbed the chain with my arm and pulled up. I tried standing but my legs were very weak. It was so dark in here my eyes could barely adjust. It smelled very musky. I wrinkled my nose the smell of that monster was still on my skin. I wondered if that was a way they tracked their prey or if they just really smelled this bad. I tried moving and the chains rattled. I didn't know where anything was or where I was.

"Ok, ok, think. You have to be able to do something. Dust, try the dust."

I rubbed my fingers together, in the dark the dust was bright and I could see a little bit of the room. It was all some kind of stone or concrete. I turned around and did it again. These chains were very large going into the wall and narrowed as it reached my wrist. I looked down at the chain and rubbed my fingers over it. The dust sprinkled over the chain.

I waited but nothing happened.

"Ok, that didn't work. I...I don't know what to do. How do I get out of here?"

I started to panic. What's going to happen to me? Why am I here?

I guess the only way to get answers is to find someone or I could wait here and maybe starve to death.

I looked around and listened. I didn't hear anyone or any movement at all. I pulled on the chains. I put my foot against the wall as far as the chain would let me go and pushed off, pulling the chains. I pulled hard over and over again until the smell of blood reached my nose. I could feel it dripping off my skin. Finally, I realized I wasn't getting out of these chains. I started to feel helpless as the warm, salty tears rolled down my face. I leaned my back against the wall, sliding down the wall till my butt hit the floor. I put my head in my hands and cried. I felt so lost and I really thought this was going to be the end. I thought I was going to die.

I opened my eyes, not realizing I had drifted off to sleep. I heard the footsteps coming down the hall. I heard the metal scraping as they inserted a key into the door. It turned and my heart sped up and the door unlocked. I stood on unsteady legs, the door opened and the smell of wet dog hit my nose. Like the Dr. at the hospital. Light entered the room; I covered my eyes from the light until they could adjust. Slowly, I moved my hands from my face and saw two men standing there looking at me with different looks of confusion and awe.

"I don't understand, the Alpha said she should have turned a few hours ago. I mean the smell was strong."

They looked at each other, "Should we get her anyway?"

"What if she can turn at will? I've never seen a she moonwalker."

The other man shook his head, "I don't think so."

I watched the men converse back and forth before they walked towards me.

I looked between the two and could see their lights, theirs were different from the others I've seen, and it was mostly green. There weren't a whole lot of mixed colors.

They walked till they were in front of me.

I backed up against the wall, "Who are you? What do you want with me?"

They looked at each other but didn't say a whole lot. They reached out and grabbed the chain. I wasn't thinking about my wrist and as soon as he pulled on it the pain came back to me.

"Awe, that hurts."

They stopped and looked down, "What did you do?"

"I woke up chained to a wall! What do you think I was doing?"

They looked taken aback by my attitude but I wasn't going to show how afraid I was.

They unchained me from the wall but kept them chained to my wrists.

"Walk rogue."

"What?"

"What's rogue?"

"I said walk."

He gave a small tug but I didn't want it to pull so I started walking. We walked for a while up some stairs to this large bright room. There was a table in the middle with two anchor hooks in the floor to hook the chains to.

"Sit down."

I walked over to the chair and sat down. They didn't say anything else just hooked my chains and walked out. I was there for what felt like forever until I finally heard the door open again. I looked up and there was this huge, like huge man walked in. It wasn't just his size but his presents filled the room of power and authority. He had to have been 6'6 or taller and had the build of a boxer. He had dark hair and skin, blue eyes and his color was blue-greenish. He, just like the others, had that nasty, wet dog smell. I almost had to hold my nose because his was worse than the others. He didn't have a very pleasant look about him. It was actually the opposite. He looked at me like I was the scum of the earth.

"You didn't think you would get caught did you? You are your filthy packs running, thinking you can take over and run other packs into the ground. Well, sweetie you picked to large of a pack to take down by yourself. However, before we kill you, I need some answers. If the answers are informative and I can use it, maybe I let you live."

My mind was totally blank. The only words I caught were 'kill me'. I didn't want to show him how afraid I was, I would not give into whatever these people wanted. I was about to object when the door opened again and a man and woman walked in. He had a bag in his hand and the woman made me feel funny on the inside. The second she looked at me she had this very odd look on her face. She didn't look like the kind of person to second guess herself but she seemed very confused. She had short blond hair, short about 5'2, and blue eyes. Her skin was light brown.

"You know, I hate to see someone as gorgeous as you be wasted away and believe me, I don't want to kill you but I can't have your kind running around."
The girl then looked at the big guy with confusion.
"First, where is your pack?"
I looked at him, "What's a pack?"

He looked at me very annoyed. He held his hand out and the man gave him the bag.

"Do you know what's in this bag?"

I shook my head.

"It's silver, keep it up."

He dropped the silver rock onto the table.

"Again, where is your pack and why are you on my territory."

I rolled my eyes and the big man in front of my made this sound. It was like growling.

"Look Mr. Guy I don't know anything about your stupid pack crap."

He looked at me like I insulted his mother. He looked back at the other guy and he grabbed the stone. He walked towards me with it and the first thing I though was he was going to hit me with it. He walked over and grabbed my arm. Fear ran through me. I couldn't help but noticed the look on the girls face. It was curiosity. My fear faded when I looked at her but I don't know why. I felt the cold stone touch my skin and I waited for him to hurt me but nothing happened. I looked at the man holding the stone and his face was very confused. He held the stone with a pair of black gloves. "What is that supposed to do?"

The big guy looked at me, "Not what I expected."

The look on his face never changed. The men looked at each other for a few minutes without saying anything. I looked in between the two, "Will someone please tell me why I am here?"

By now the girl has walked over and stood behind me.

"Alpha, if I may can I ask her a few questions?"

He looked at her like this was not in the ordinary.

"Alpha, what kind of name is that?"

He looked at me but didn't say anything. After a few minutes of staring at each other he looked at the girl and nodded. She smiled and I could feel her excitement.

"So what do you know about your species?"

I looked at her, "Like whatever this clown is talking about or my species?" I pointed to myself. The 'Alpha' made the growling noise again.

"And what the heck are you doing." I looked at the Alpha.

"His wolf is growling." The girl answered me. I looked at her and as terrified as I was I wanted to just laugh.

"His wolf, I'm sorry I don't understand."

She looked at me with curiosity.

"He is a werewolf."

I stood up and backed away from him. The only experience I have ever had with anything that looked like a wolf was the one that attacked me and the flashbacks hit me at the word wolf. His ugly face lit up in my mind and I cringed.

"Sit down"

I heard his voice but still only see that thing, that monster.

"I said SIT!" the Alpha commanded.

I could hear the command in his tone but my body was not forced to obey like the others. As soon as the word left his mouth the man behind him hit the floor.

"I'm not your puppet! You think I'm going to listen to you when you freaks attacked me in the first place. I still can't get rid of its stench."

The alpha stood, "Take her down and get rid of her. We aren't getting any information."

"Wait, Alpha please. Didn't you hear her, I know you are upset over what happened but you are jumping too quickly.

I know it's not my place to say but you are wrong about her. She isn't one of them. Look at the evidence. Silver didn't burn her, she doesn't follow your command, and obviously she doesn't know what you're talking about. Why don't you give her a chance to talk and tell us where she came from and why she has the stench of a moonwalker?"

"That was supposed to burn me?" I asked offended. "And what's a moonwalker? Is that what attacked me?"

The girl looked at me, "Something attacked you?"

"Besides you people, yes. I was walking and I smelled that same disgusting smell I did at the hospital with the man and the claws and I just started running and it tackled me and tried to...do something but I don't know what it was."

The Alpha stopped me, "Man with claws? You can see the moonwalker in original form and if it attacked you how did you get away? Hardly even we wolves can escape if we are alone."

"I don't know he just ran off."

The alpha snorted.

I stood up annoyed with his ego, "You know for being so sure of yourself, you don't see the picture very clearly. I was attacked by that monster and then by your mutts that smell like a bunch of wet dogs. Then, you let your anger get to you and only smell that monsters slime on me and don't even realize I'm not one of them. You owe me an apology buddy."

He stood and snarled lunging towards me. I jumped back but held my ground. I don't know where this bravery came from but it sure wasn't me. He didn't say anything and walked out stopping by the man who was sitting behind him. They starred a few seconds and he was gone.

The man looked at me shaking his head, "For someone who is so tiny, you have a lot of spunk. My name is Bain that was Alpha Brian. You have to excuse him; we have been through a lot. His mate was hurt badly by the same monsters you say attacked you. You are the only person that so far has survived with only minor injuries. If we can figure out how you escaped maybe we can figure out how to find a weak spot."

He looked at me and shrugged his shoulders.

"What's a mate?"

He looked up at me and smiled, "A mate is the one person who will love you no matter what. Like, do you believe in true love or love at first site?"

I shrugged, "Never really thought about it but I guess I could."

He nodded, "Well, our wolves will know who their mate is by their smell, or by making eye contact. Them both wolves will connect and they will be lifelong partners. If one is not a wolf, then it can get complicated."

"Oh"

The girl behind me clapped her hands together, "Ok, so we have so much to talk about, I'm so excited."

I looked at her and smiled. She looked back up at Bain, "If you don't mind, could you guard us from the outside."

He smiled and rolled his eyes, "Whatever, have your girl talk."

"Ok", she looked at me, "What kind of fairy are you. I can feel the vibes rolling off you so you must be higher up in

the ranks. I've never met a fairy like that. Oh I can't wait to
have fairy talk....."
She went on for what seemed like forever, were all fairies
like this. If she can feel me, I bet that's what that feeling
was when she entered the room. I'm not a fairy though?
Could I actually tell her what I was? Maybe this could be
good and I could actually find out more about me.
She was still jabbering on about I have no idea what.
"Actually", she stopped and looked at me, "I'm not a fairy."
She looked at me confused, "But, I can feel..."
I looked at her; I was putting on my faith in a few words. I
breathed out one good time, here goes nothing.

"I'm not a fairy, I'm a pixie."

Chapter 8

"You people need to get out of my house...NOW!"
"You tell us where the girl is and we will be on our way."
"I already told you, I'm not telling you anything."
"Fine, we'll do this the hard way."
These large men just barged in looking for Macy. There
were four of them and they were all very build and had
scars on their faces. I wasn't going to let them in the house
but they didn't give me a chance to close the door. I tried
closing it but they were way too strong for me.
"What do you want with my daughter in the first place?"
"That would be none of your business."
Rage flew through me, "None....NONE of MY
BUSINESS! SHE IS MY DAUGHTER!"

One of the men turned around with an ugly sly smile,
"Now, now Mrs. Ryan. We both know that's a lie, don't
we."

"Mom, what's he talking about?"

I turned around to see Sage, one of my younger boys
standing behind me. I never told them how I actually came
to have Macy. Yes, it's true I didn't actually give birth to
her but I raised her to be my own since she was an infant. I
will never forget when I held her for the first time. She was
so tiny and was the most beautiful baby I had ever seen but
after a few minutes I knew something was very different
about her. Her platinum blond hair and green eyes was very

odd. Something you don't see very often around here. Her skin was like porcelain, she was beautiful. This family said she was in danger and needed her to be adopted by a 'different' kind of family. I never asked any questions. Maybe I should have. When Macy was five I gave a small seed for her to plant. We went outside, dug a small hole, and put the seed in with some water. She stood over the spot where we planted the flower and she waited.

"Honey, it takes time for these things to grow."

She smiled and raised her hand over the shoveled dirt, "No, mama watch this."
She rubbed her thumb and fingers together and this golden sparkly dust fell and I starred in awe. The flower grew and bloomed in seconds. It bloomed bright and was the most beautiful flower I had ever seen.
I looked at my daughter and knew this had to be kept a secret, I don't know why but I knew I had to. She was very special and this is why that family didn't want her.

"Sweetie, this is beautiful...but you can't do this kind of stuff. You can never do this and you must forget you can do this. I drilled this into her head over and over until one day I think she really did forget and I raised her as a regular human child. Her being as pretty as she was did attract a little bit of attention. People were always asking for me to enroll her in pageants but I wanted her life to be normal as possible. I didn't know keeping everything from her was going to put her into so much danger. Now our family is being torn apart and theses men are searching for my daughter.

"Alright boys, she isn't here. Let's go."

I watched them walk out leaving my home is ruble. I followed them to the door and listened as the talked outside.

"Keep this home under tabs until she arrives. I don't care how long it takes I want that girl, alive."

The other man nodded and they all walked off but I knew one would be close by.

"Mom who were those men and what do they want with Macy?"

"Lacy."

I turned to see Danny walking in the door and seeing the house in shambles. He stopped and took a breath taking in the view.

"What the....who...what happened?"

"Danny these men came looking for Macy."

"Why, what did they want with her? Where is she?"

I shrugged my shoulders, feeling so helpless not being able to have any answers.

"No one knows."

"Mom, what is going on?"

I turned around to Sage, Aden, and Abby. I sighed looking at my husband Danny.

"Can we all sit down please?"

We turned out couch back over and everyone sat down around me.

"I never found out what exactly what she was, but I wanted her to feel normal. I didn't want everyone to look at her like she was some kind of freak. Then, the hospital accident happened and the doctor wanted to know what she was because he knew she wasn't human. I just knew my secret was going to get out. The night Macy left; she left a note. I pulled the letter out and handed it to my kids and husband. Everyone looked at it then back to me.
"You never told us about this. Why?"

sniffle
"I'm really sorry I never told any of you but I couldn't allow the truth to get out. Now it has anyway and it's my entire fault."
I looked down at my hands as the tears ran down my face. The tears dripped on my sleeves and my husband reached up wiping my face.

"We need to find out why they want our daughter and that she is safe. I dot care if she isn't ours or that's she is different. She is MY daughter too."
Everyone nodded but was still taking in what I said. Sage looked at me with disbelief.
"Mom, so you're telling me, Macy wasn't a human but some kind of mythical creature and you didn't tell us because you thought we would tell people?"
I nodded, "More or less, yes."
"Ok."
I rubbed Sage's head and looked up noticing someone was missing.
"Where's Tanner?"

Everyone looked around. I jumped up, "Tanner!"
I called but there was no response. Everyone jumped up
and started searching.
"Tanner!! Tanner!!"
We searched the entire house but he was nowhere to be
found.
"Was he here earlier?" Danny asked.

"No, he said he was going to Andrew's house for the
night." Sage answered him.

Aden looked at Sage, "That's not true I was over there to
Drew's to drop off his game system and Tanner wasn't
there."

I just sat down, "Ok there isn't a reason to panic yet. There
could be a good reason why he would lie. Maybe he was
mistaken, did anyone call his phone?"
"On it now," Aden puts his phone to his ear. He let it ring
till the voicemail came up, "Hey Tanner, call us ASAP it's
important." Aden hung up the phone and looked at me.

KNOCK

We all looked at the door. I stood but Danny gestured that I
sit. Danny grabbed his 38 from the desk drawer. He walked
to the door and cracked it open.
"Oh thank you Lord."
He opened the door to Abby. She walked in and froze at the
sight of us and the condition of the house.
"What happened here?"

No one really said anything till I spoke up, "Macy is gone and Tanner is gone. These men came and ransacked the house looking for Macy or where she would be. I don't know why they want her or who they were. My son is gone, my daughter is gone and I don't know if they are even alive."

"What do you mean gone? You think something happened to them?"

We sat Abby down and filled her in on everything that has happened; Macy's note and Tanner lying. I told her bits and pieces about Macy and Abby seemed to think I was crazy but she didn't say anything.

"What would they want with Macy? DO you think Tanner leaving is related?" Abby questioned me. I shrugged my shoulders. I just didn't know.

"Has anyone called the cops?" Abby looked at me. I shook my head.

"Why?"

I looked at Abby, "This is a lot more complicated than that. If they are looking for her for a certain reason and if the cops are looking for her it will make their jobs a lot easier. I can't put her in danger more than I already have."

"Abby looked at me, "Are you kidding me? You're not going to call the cops because you think Macy is some witch and these big guys are looking for her. What sense does that make? She isn't magic and we need to call the cops now."

Abby picked her phone, "Abby no. If you do this you might as well kiss you sister goodbye. Please just wait and we will find someone that can find her and not be so open about it."

Abby didn't seem happy about it but she put the phone down.

"I can't believe this crap." She walked out of the house.

"Let's straighten this up." I stood and started moving stuff. It took us a while but we finally got things back in order. I went to Tanners room and sat on his bed. Macy's room was just down the hall.

Tanner, come back home.

Chapter 9

She didn't say anything for what seemed like an eternity. She just looked at me with wide eyes and her mouth agape. She had the look of awe and terror in her blue eyes. Her tan skin turned a pale white and I could feel the emotions rolling off her. She closed her mouth and opened it again trying to find something to say.

"T…that's impossible...they've been extinct for over a hundred years."

She stood up and stepped away from me. I didn't understand. My smile turned to a frown, "That's how I got away from the scary wolf thing."

She looked at me, "You fought hit off?"

"No, I used pixie dust. (I still wanted to giggle) He was on top of me and he had his tongue out slobbering everywhere and I threw pixie dust in his face."

She had the look of awe, "He was slobbering on you? He didn't bite you?"

I shook my head.

"Oh no....oh no..." She started pacing back and forth, "I need to talk to Bain."

"Wait!" I jumped up, "You can't tell anyone about me."

She froze, "Why not? You're like the last of your kind; that I have ever heard of and you don't want me to say anything?"

"Because what if someone is looking for me like the girl at the beach said; she told me we were hunted to the point of extinction and I should never tell anyone what I am and I just told you."

At this point I could feel my own fear swell up in my belly, "Bad people will look and if the word gets out what I am. Your family and all these people could be in danger. You should have never brought me here. They should have left me in the woods where they found me."

She stopped and thought about it, "Whoever would be after you...I guess you're right."
"Well, because of what I am, I know people will hunt me. Just like the rest of my kind."
She nodded, "I do need to tell him about the moonwalker's actions though. It's very odd." I nodded and she poked her head out the door. Seconds later Bain comes rushing back in. He listens to what the fairy had to say while throwing confused glances at me every now and then, "Oh man is this crazy. So can you tell me exactly what happened?"
I went over the details of my attack with Bain and he didn't really say anything just nodded here and there. Finally, I was done telling him what happen, (minus the pixie dust part).
"So one of the moonwalkers has favored you? That's the weirdest thing I have ever heard. This is crazy; I don't understand how you got away from him. He didn't want to hurt you just...well." He chuckles under his breath, "I'm going to talk to the Alpha."
He nodded goodbye and opened the door walking out. I looked to the girl, "Uh...I never got your name."
"Oh my gosh. How rude of me. I can't believe I didn't tell you my name yet. I'm Beth, I'm a war fairy, that's the only reason these wolves keep a fairy around." She giggled, "We have been able to defeat all kinds of threats except for these

moonwalkers." She looked down at her hands. "I can't beat them."

I looked at her and she seems so vulnerable when she doubted herself... She looked up at me and I smiled.

"If it makes you feel any better, I was raised by humans and you're the first person like me I have ever really met. I know nothing about me or being a pixie."

She wrinkled her eyebrows, "Then, how do you know what you are?"

"Oh ..."

I went on to tell her about the girl I met when I was little that I mentioned earlier.

"What else do you remember?" Beth asked.

I looked her and frowned, "Not a lot. I just discovered all this a few months ago when I started blacking out."

"Blacking out? What caused them?"

I shrugged, "No one knows yet."

She was about to say something when the door opened and the Alpha walked back in.

"You," The Alpha pointed at me, "Let's go."

Fear swelled up in my stomach again. I looked at Beth and she nodded. I got up and followed the Alpha out the door and down this really long hallway. The walls were bare, all dull white. I think the wolves could kind of feel my fear because Bain would throw me a reassuring glance every now and then. Didn't help much though, the Alpha never paid me any mind, he just kept walking. As I followed I could start to hear moving and heavy breathing. I turned my ears in the direction we were heading, "What's that noise?"

The Alpha turned to me, "You can here that now?"

I nodded, "Mhmm."

The Alpha turned around and kept walking forward. He's not the warmest person I might add.

We continued walking for a few more minutes and the noise got louder and clearer. It was growling and snarling it was terrifying. I scooted closer to Beth and she held my hand. We ended up in front of a large metal door with a huge lock. There were cell bars on top where you could see through. The Alpha stepped aside and motions for me to come forward. I nervously stepped forward and looked at the Alpha.

"Look inside." I nodded, and tried to peer inside but I wasn't tall enough.

I looked at the Alpha again and he huffed but sent Bain to grab me a stool. I couldn't help but notice the Alpha noticing when Beth giggled. Bain came back in a few seconds and I stood on the stool peering through the steel bars. The stench hit my nose again and it was worse this time because the creature was in a confined room. I help my nose, "But, it stinks really badly."

The Alpha looked at me with a look I wasn't too sure about but motioned for me to continue so I did. I looked over and saw a very large wolf like creature sitting in the corner. It was chained the wall with large silver chains. As soon as I came into view the creature looked up and saw me. His eyes went from boredom to intense excitement in seconds. He jumped up and tried to reach me but stepped back when the silver pulled on his skin. He whined and pleaded, wanting to reach me. He looked devastated.

"Would you go in?" The Alphas voice cut in.

I looked at the Alpha my face blank, "I...I. Don't know."

He looked at Bain, who then stuck the key in the door and turned it. They both looked at me but waited before they unlocked it. I stared into space, thinking what if it attacks me? Would they save me? Finally, I looked up at Bain and nodded. I stepped down off the stool. I stepped back and it felt like it was an eternity before the door opened.

"Ahum."

I looked at the Alpha who was waiting for me to enter. I looked ahead and the room seemed darker than before. I took a step, my hands shook and I could feel my heart beating through my chest. The beast whimpered as I got closer and I seem to be less afraid. Finally, I was close enough where I could reach out and touch its smelly skin. He reached out and brushed my skin with his large paw. It was clammy and rough but didn't hurt. Now that I was within reach he calmly sat down and waited for me to say something.

"Umm Hi."

He nodded back to be.

"Can you understand her?"

I jumped not seeing the Alpha come in behind me. My nerves were already frayed from today's events.

My heart pounded and I heard a terrifying growl. I looked behind me and the beast had grown four times his size into this massive wolf creature. Fear ripped through me and I felt like my heart was going to burst, my face paled, and breathing hitched. I jumped to the Alpha and grabbed his arm. I knew he wouldn't like it because he hates me as it is.

I had never felt so alone than this moment. The Alpha
looked at me and looked at the beast.
"Look, your scarring her to death!"
The monster turned to me and his eyes met mine. He
reached out and I tried to move but my body wouldn't
budge. He reached out but didn't fully make contact with
my skin.
"Beast, can you understand her?" His ears twitched to the
Alphas voice but the beast never looks away from me. I
blinked a few times and got myself under control releasing
the Alphas arm.
"Will you ask this dumb animal the question?"
The Alpha looked at me and I nodded.
"Can you understand me?"
The beast nodded again.
I had to look way up because of how much it had grown.
"Can you shrink back down so my neck doesn't have to
hurt so badly?"
He looked at the Alpha and back to me again. He gave the
Alpha a dirty scowl causing the Alpha to growl and the
beast growled back.
I thought they were going to start fighting and I didn't want
to be in the middle of it. I looked at the beast, "This man
won't hurt me" I reached out a shaky hand and touched the
monsters belly to make him look at me. The beast gave in
and shrank back then sat down.
"Can we give it a bath or something?" I held my nose and
the beast turned its head smelling itself. He didn't seem
dissatisfied and lay down at my feet.
"Ok, I have seen enough."

The Alpha turned around walking out, I followed but not before hearing the whining from the upset beast. I turned around to see his saddened face.

"It's ok beast, I'll be back."

He nodded and sat awaiting my return.

We walked down the hall entering this room with a large, brown table and many chairs. "Sit."

The Alpha commanded and everyone sat except me. I didn't feel the command the others felt. I looked around at which chair I wanted to sit in and saw a spinning one. The Alpha watched me as I walked behind him and grabbed the small chair and sat down at the table.

The Alpha cleared his throat, "I have a few concerns I would like to bring up. One, we know nothing about you or where you come from, you don't feel the need to follow my commands, your manners are far from adequate, and I don't know how well you can be trusted.

I huffed, "If that's number one, jeez. I'd hate to hear number two..."

"That's what I'm talking about. I am the Alpha here and you have no respect for authority."

"That's because you're a big meanie and you haven't said one nice thing to me."

He looked taken aback, opening and closing his mouth a few times, not knowing how to answer the comment.

"Two," He went on, "The beasts seem to like and understand you and only you. This is very unsettling to me and also very useful. I shall hold a pack meeting tonight to see what your future holds.

"My future, what's that supposed to mean?" Everyone in the room seemed to be as surprised as myself. "Look

Alpha, I don't know what kind of rules you go by but you hold nothing of my future. You brought me here; I didn't come here on my own. So you either let me stay or let me go."

I looked straight at the Alpha and he smiled, with actually scared me more.

"Then tell me the truth, tell me what you are and how you escaped the moonwalker before."

The Alpha stood over me with his hands on my chair arms. His dark eyes were intense and full of anger, "Don't lie this time, your life depends on it."

Chapter 10

I stared into the Alphas eyes, "I just found out werewolves are real, seriously?"

The Alpha looked at me and smirked, "The meeting will be at twelve noon. Don't be late." He nodded to Bain and walked out of the room. Bain now had this "I'm sorry" look on his face.

"Sorry Macy, but I have to put you in one of the lockdown rooms since the Alpha thinks you are a flight risk. Well of course I was, I wanted out of there.

"No funny business though." I nodded and followed the Bain and the guard across the hallway. He opened the door and I walked in, closing the door behind me. I lay there on the bed looking at the walls since that was the only thing I could look at. There were no windows or others door except the bathroom. Maybe a nice hot shower will help me think. I mean I do smell like a moonwalker still. I lock the door, which didn't matter from what I saw those wolves could break the door down if they wanted to. I turn the shower on and turn it hot and slowly climbed under the hot water. I lay down in the bathtub after shampooing with the "guest" shampoo. My hair had grown so long and was now almost to my butt so combing this out was going to be fun since I didn't have any conditioner. I laid there letting the hot water fall over me, feeling warmth from the water and the sound made me start to drift off.

BANG

I jumped from the noise, realizing I was still in the bathtub and the water was now ice cold. I got out and grabbed a towel wrapping in around me.

"Hello?"

"It's about freaking time." A very mad Bain yelled through the other side, "I was about to break the door down. I brought you some pajamas from Beth and clothes for in the morning. I'll leave them on the bed."

"Ok, uh…thank you."

"Yep." Is all I head before the door to the bedroom closed. I stood looking in the mirror. I looked tired with bags under my eyes. I could imagine I have been running on very little sleep since I ran away. I thought about Bain breaking in here and seeing me…well naked. I looked in the mirror and I had a very curvy body but I didn't want anyone else to see just yet. I glanced at the mirror before I grabbed the clothes and I saw my body glisten. Like a light shimmered over it. I stopped and looked in the mirror again. I felt he fear coming back, I still hadn't gotten used to all these changes yet and how they have negatively affected my life. I focused on my skin and felt it tingle; light glistened starting from my head, going down to my toes. As the light traveled my skin turned to this rugged texture and my nipples disappeared, my breasts tightened, I looked down and you couldn't see anything. It was like, like a barbie doll almost. There was like, no "body parts" visible. I ran my hands down my skin and it was tough and rugged. I looked into the mirror again my pointy ears were more visible and my eyes were a brighter green. I was strangely beautiful. I was terrified. I closed my eyes. "Please go back to normal, please go back to normal." I felt the strange but familiar feeling again. I cracked open one eye and I was normal again.

"Thank you." I whispered to myself. I wished I could just be normal. I put on the pajamas and lay in the bed. My thoughts drifted to what I used to be, how normal everything was and Bruce. He was a hottie, gay as he may have been. He was also my best friend but I knew I would be giving all that up when I ran away. I closed my eyes again and again trying to fall asleep. Maybe I should show up tomorrow? Could I find a way out of here? I had to think this through, tomorrow if they find I should be killed I will be heavily guarded. Right now I could…

Knock, Knock, Knock

My thoughts were interrupted. The knocking was so quiet if it wasn't for my advanced hearing I would have never heard it. I looked at the clock and it was two AM. Who would be knocking on my door at two in the morning? I stood up and all the hair on my skin stood up. All the sudden goose bumps ran from my head to my toes. I grabbed the handle and twisted opening the door. I stuck my head out and Beth barged in with Bain behind her. They both looked at me with wide eyes. Beth was giving me a look and I could understand what it was. Bain's eyes travel down my body and I looked down and realized my skin had changed.

"I can explain, Bain, I…"

"Don't, I don't need to know." I looked confused and I looked to Beth.

"You need to get out now. The Alpha, he wants to use you. We both told him he can't but with everything that has happened he is losing it. He wants to create an army with the beasts and use them to fight the neighboring packs. He wants all control and will do anything to get it."

"You're just going to let me go against your Alpha's orders?" I looked at them with disbelief.

"Well, no." I backed up, "No not like that. We're going with you."

I looked at them, "Why, your Alpha will be mad. Won't he?"

Bain huffed, "Mad isn't the word. He will be furious. He will come after you and I don't know for how long but we have wanted to get out for a while now. We just have never had a good enough reason to leave the pack. Once you are accepted by an Alpha you have to have his permission to leave or have a valid reason to leave the pack. If not, when your caught you can be considered for execution. This way we will just be rouges."

"Rogue that's what you and the Alpha kept calling me. What is that?"

"A rogue is a lone wolf. He doesn't belong to a pack."

I nodded, "Why are you helping me? You're putting yourself in more danger trying to help me."

Bain looked at Beth and they smiled at each other, "Bain is my true mate and the Alpha wouldn't approve because of my species. He doesn't believe is contaminating the bloodline."

"Mates, wolves, moonwalkers, pixies, this is all too much for one day."

"Pixie?" Bain looked at me, "Those don't even exist." He laughed shaking his head. Me and Beth shared a smile and rolled our eyes.

"Anyway, in thirty minutes there are going to be a distraction allowing us to escape. Don't ask I don't have the time to explain. The distraction will give us about three minutes to get out of the pack house and ten two get off the territory. Beth can get you out faster because she can get above the tree tops and stay out of site. She will carry you. Put these clothes on and wait till you hear the commotion. Beth will take you out the window and over the tree tops." I nodded and Bain took off out the door. I put on the black skinny jeans, black top, and a large black beanie to put all my blond hair in. My skin had tanned since I have been in the woods so my blond hair stands out. Beth stayed with me and Bain took off out the door waiting to cause the distraction. While we waited Beth and I started backing everything we would need. We only had thirty minutes and we will have to travel light so we had to make fast decisions. I grabbed my clothes and anything that could be used to start a fire. Beth snuck out and grabbed soaps, more clothes, and any food she could find. She came back by the door and we snuck into the next room since the room I had didn't have a window. We waited to hear the ruckus. It had been about twenty minutes so it should be about any minute now.

(Incoherent yelling)

"That's got to be the distraction." Beth looked at me and we both nodded. We stood on the window seal together and took one last look at each other before we jumped. She got behind me and grabbed me from the back.

"Humph"

I was jerked forward when her wings opened. I looked up and could see her giant, clear-ish, white wings spreading, catching the wind as we flew. It was the most amazing feeling ever. They were long about a six foot wingspan with glistening feathers. She turned them and they reflected the color of the clouds so we blended in with whatever was in the sky, which right now was not good. They were dark clouds with roaring thunder. We didn't feel the heavy gusts of wind or rain yet so that was a good thing. We just needed to get out of sight. I looked down to look for Bain but I didn't see him yet. I hope he is alright. We flew for a good while until the wind picked up ruffling through Beth's feathers making it hard for her to fly. We would get jerked around or one of her wings would fold above us and we would tumble down till she got control again. I felt the first drop of rain of my arms and I looked up. The sky was almost black and I could barely see anything around me. "We're going to have to land!" Beth yelled down to me. Her voice was shaky as she struggles to keep control. She tilted her wings and we began to glide down towards the dark forest.

"I'm trying to wait for a clearing so we don't get hurt landing!"

I could barely hear her voice with the wind swooshing by my ears. The rain was soaking Beth's wings making them heavy and hard to maneuver. A large gust blew through and Beth's wing folded in mid-air, "Hold on Macy!!"

I folded my arms in and tucked my knees. I rubbed my hands together trying to make the dust but my hands were so wet I couldn't. We were now in a dive towards the ground and I knew the impact would be hard. I had to slow us down. I unfolded my arms and let the heat run through me and pushed with everything I had. The wing hit the ground and came back up hitting us and Beth's wings opening them back up. I kept pushing till she regained control and could slow the fall. I knew she would have to

tuck her wings again or risk the trees tearing them apart but
I would wait till I was closer. Finally the tree tops were
only feet below me and I rubbed my hands together hard. I
felt the dust building and I through it below us. We went
through it and Beth tucked her wings around us both. The
dust slowed us down right before we hit the ground and we
landed somewhat safely. We hit the ground with a thumb
and rolled into the leaves. Beth stood and wobbled a little
her body was weak from the energy she used to keep us
alive. I stood next neither of us were seriously injured just
some scraped and bruises. The only bad thing is its still
pouring rain and everything we have is soaked or ruined.
"Are you ok?"
Beth nodded to me and I walked over to her and put her
arm around my shoulder.
"We need to find somewhere to get out of the rain!" Beth
yelled to me over the sound of the rain and thunder. I
nodded in agreement and we started to walk through the
woods. We walked for about thirty minutes till we found a
tree that hard very large leaves we could use to make a
water proof roof. I sat Beth down on the soft ground and
began to pull the leaves down. Nothing would be dry
enough to make a fire but we would have to find a way to
keep warm. It's not too cold but the rain will send us into a
hypothermic state. Beth was already starting to shiver. I
grabbed some limbs and put them in between two trees to
make a roof. I also placed bigger logs under them to make a
bed. I tried to find something to soften the logs. Everything
was so wet from the rain. I needed to find a way to start a
fire. I looked over and Beth was shivering pulling her knees
into her chest trying to stay warm. I felt myself begin to

panic I didn't know what to do. I grabbed some moss up and started putting it on the logs. Something sticky got on my hand I grabbed some wet moss and rubbed it on my hands to try to get the sap off. I was getting angrier with myself by the minute. It was like one thing after another, nothing could go right. I felt the tears of frustration leave my eyes mixing with the rain dripping down my face.

"This is bull-crap!" I stood up throwing the moss on the ground, "It's not fair." I stomped the ground and the heat flowed through me. I pushed the heat out and away from me. I stood there standing wiping the tears away. Beth scooted closer to me, "How do you do that?"

I looked down at her, "What?"

"Look." She pointed up and that's when I realized I wasn't getting wet. I had pushed a bubble out around us that the rain couldn't penetrate. It landed on the outside and rolled off like an umbrella.

"I don't know. I was feeling so angry that I got us all into this I zone out."

She nodded, "So when you show a great amount of emotion usually you find a new talent. Sometimes it takes that much energy and emotion to find your limits." She smiled up at me.

"Hey, now maybe I can get some of this moss dry."

I sat down and grabbed a handful of wet moss and sat in in my bubble.

"Maybe you can dry it? Like when you used the wind to open my wings."

Beth shivers

"I'll try but that was when stuff just happens I don't mean to do them it's like instinct takes over and I sum how know what to do. I don't know how to do it I think about it."

She laughs, "Then don't think about it. Just imagining it happening and do it."

I looked at the moss and tried to think of it dry. I sat there for a few moments but nothing happened. I put my hands over it and imagine the moss getting hot and drying out. I pushed with everything is my body but I didn't feel anything.

I sighed and Beth shivered again. I knew I had to do this I had to make her warm. I looked at the moss again and tried to concentrate. I finally felt the heat building inside me again. I pushed outward feeling it flow through my chest to my arm and out my fingers. The moss begins to turn from a wet, green and black to a light brown and frizzled look. I pushed harder till my hands felt like they were going to catch on fire. Smoke started drifting from the moss till a small spark ignited. I laughed and the feeling of joy flowed through me. The fire grew and busted into flames. We jumped back and looked at each other and laughed. I grabbed few more handfuls and some sticks to. A few minutes later Beth and I were snuggled in front of the fire. I pushed the bubble farther until our make-shift hut was out of the rain and drying out as well. I sat and stared into the fire wondering of how I was capable of all this the whole time and never knew it. I looked at Beth; finally now I have someone I can share it with. Someone who understands me for what I am. The bubble helped keep the heat in so I lay down and slowing closed my eyes letting the warmth and the comfort of a friend send me into the arms of the night.

SNAP*CRACKLE

The sound of the fire woke e. I slowly opened my eyes letting the light in. It was still very dark outside by the point of the moon I would say around three in the morning. I looked over at Beth who was still sounding asleep. I stepped out of the bubble to get more wood to dry out before our fire died.

SNAP

I jerked my head up. That was not the sound of the fire. I snipped the air and caught the scent of someone but I didn't recognize it. I grabbed one of the sticks I had picked up for the fore and help it in the ready position in case I had to use it.

CRACK

Another twig snapped to the left of me and I caught the scent of another. I was not alone.

"Hey!"

I jumped, "Beth you scared the freaking crap out of me!"

She laughed but soon noticed my expression was not of fun and jokes.

"What do you see?"

"Nothing but I hear and smell them."

"Them?"

I nodded, "We need to get back to the hut. Now!"

We both turned and as we did we heard the crashing of something large headed towards us. I could hear the heavy breathing and panting of whatever it was. The bubble was just ahead Beth and I entered the bubble and hid in out hut. Hoping we were camouflage enough that we wouldn't be noticed. All the noise stopped and we saw two large wolves enter the small area we cleared. They looked around and one liked right at us and I froze. Our eyes locked for what seemed like an eternity. He then just turned and looked the other way as if he didn't even notice I was there. They sniffed the air and the ground around us but never once did they get led in our direction.

"Can they not see us?" Beth whispered to me. I looked at her and shrugged my shoulders. Eventually they seemed satisfied and wondered off into the same woods they came from. I was finally able to relax. It was my turn to sleep so Beth stood watch while I slept.

Everything was so big and tall. I felt like I was only two inches tall. The wind whipped around me and I was being pushed around like a rag doll. I ran and tried to escape the wind but something on my back kept getting snagged. I turned around and was shocked at what I saw. There were wings on my back bright red like fire long with jagged edges. It looked like there were holes but when I reached to touch them I felt nothing but softness underneath my fingers. There were no holes and I reached out with my hand to feel the edges.

Oh, they were tough, spiny, and sharp. I looked back at my hands and there was blood dripping from a cut on my hand. It healed right before my eyes. I looked up and the grass was taller than I was. The trees looked like they touched the sky. All the bugs were as big as I was. I didn't know what was going on or where I was. I walked over to large tree trying not to fall over from the wind pushing me finally the wind left as I stepped behind this large tree. I looked down and fear filled my eyes. Everything I looked at started to die right before my eyes. The leaves and grass all turned brown and withered. I reached out and touched it.

FIRE

Fire erupted from my finger torching everything in my path. I looked down at my hands and backed up. I turned and started running but the fire wasn't far behind. The wind pushed the fire, spreading it faster than I could run. It was everywhere and it was my entire fault. I felt the heat on my back and I looked behind me and my wings erupted in fire. It spread all over me and all I could see was red. All the animals were running or hiding but the ones that couldn't have to face the fire and burn to death. I screamed, "No, NOOO." I ran to the animals and they feared me running away and the more I moved the faster the fire spread. It got higher and higher I felt like I was being crushed by the fire and there was so much death.
"Stop it, make it go away!"
"Macy, wake up."
I heard my name over the blazing fire, "MACY! Wake up."

My eyes jolted open to the sight of Beth hovering over me. I sat up and my clothes stuck to my body from the sweat.
"Oh my gosh are you ok? You were screaming and thrashing around."
I looked around the room, "There's no fire?"
Beth shook her head, "No Macy, no fire."
I touched my hand to my forehead and I was burning up.
"I'm gonna get some air."
I stood up and everything started to spin.

"Do you need some help?" Beth asked me as I reached out to catch my balance.

I shook my head, "I just stood up to fast."

Finally everything became still and I walked outside our tent. That was the weirdest dream I have ever had and my only dream lately. I have been sleeping dreamlessly for months and now I'm burning forests down.

SNAP

I jerked my head towards the noise and watched intently waiting for any sign of movement. Out of the corner of my eye I see a man's figure coming through the trees. I look around for a place to hide and see a small shrub to my left. I quickly move behind it and place a shield over me. The man comes out of the shadows, "Bain!!"

Beth screams from behind me and I jump cause the bush to move. I see Bain glance over in my direction but I knew he can't see me.

"Are you ok?" He looks back at Beth as she speaks, "Yes, I am fine."

He looks behind her and back at me and sniff the air, "Where's Macy?"

Beth shrugged, "Probably back at camp come on."

He walked by me but I could tell by his posture I had him on alert. Finally after he was out of my sight I stood waiving my hand to get rid of the shield and I follow behind. Beth and Bain reach camp and I arrive a few moments after them. "Oh there you are. I was looking for you. Look who decided to show up."

I looked at Bain who then nods to me.

"It's about time I'm starving." Beth laughs at my comment and Bain rolls his eyes. He drops a sack he was holding and grabbed another bag throwing it to me. I open it up and smile at the sight of food. I grabbed a biscuit and shove it in my mouth. These aren't regular biscuits these are like hard survival biscuits. They are hard and you usually eat them with water or berries in a pot to soften them. They are really good and can last for weeks. My jaw was hurting as I chewed but I was so hungry I didn't care.

"We need to move camp. They will notice we are gone after everything calms down and will canvass a large perimeter. We need to move and get near water. There will be a more abundance of food."

Beth and I nodded and started packing what little stuff we had. I grabbed some small sticks in case we didn't have dry wood for a… fire. I shivered at the word.

"Where did you guys sleep?"

I looked at Beth and forgot he couldn't see the hut we built. I waited till he looked else ware and waved my hand removing the shield.

"Bain, it's right there."

I acted as if it was visible the whole time.

"No, no that was not there all along, I looked." Beth and I laughed at our secret but I knew since he was Beth's mate he was stuck with us. So his finding out was inevitable but for now the less people that knew the better.

www.ingramcontent.com/pod-product-compliance
Lightning Source LLC
Chambersburg PA
CBHW030529260626
47157CB00005B/1939